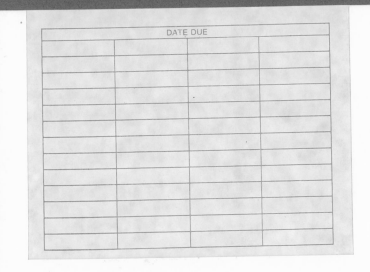

DATE DUE

F
SEN

Senisi, Ellen B.

**Just kids : visiting
a class for children
with special needs**

Just Kids

VISITING a CLASS for CHILDREN with SPECIAL NEEDS

ELLEN B. SENISI

Dutton Children's Books • New York

FOR TWO VERY SPECIAL PEOPLE:
MY SISTER BETH AND JANICE MONAGHAN.
WITHOUT THEM, THIS BOOK WOULD NOT
HAVE COME TO LIFE.

Special thanks to those who helped with the many details of this book: the nine children with special needs in this class and their parents for letting us share their lives (especially Ashley); the many adults and children at Yates Arts-in-Education Magnet School in Schenectady, New York, who helped in some way with the creation of this book (especially Cindy); Nathan Naparstek, Ph.D., and Zvi Kloppott, M.D., for expert advice on the manuscript; and Susan Van Metre for an incredible editing job.

Library of Congress Cataloging-in-Publication Data
Senisi, Ellen B.
Just kids / by Ellen B. Senisi.—1st ed.   p.   cm.
Summary: Fourth-grader Cindy is assigned to spend part of each day in the class for students with special needs, where she finds out that even though some kids may learn differently or have different abililies, they are all "just kids."
ISBN 0-525-45646-5
[1. Learning disabilities—Fiction.   2. Handicapped—Fiction.   3. Special education—Fiction.   4. Schools—Fiction.   5. Prejudices—Fiction.]   I. Title.
PZ7.s4726Ju   1998   [Fic]—dc21   97-21364   CIP   AC

Published in the United States 1998 by Dutton Children's Books,
a division of Penguin Putnam Books for Young Readers,
345 Hudson Street, New York, New York 10014
Designed by Amy Berniker
Printed in Hong Kong   First Edition
10 9 8 7 6 5 4 3

What were the other kids doing? Ashley really wanted to know. She moved closer and closer.

"Hey! Don't touch me!" said one of the girls.

Ashley's hand snapped back.

"You've got bugs—you're in the retard class," the girl shouted.

"Cindy!" exclaimed the girl's teacher. "What did you say?"

But Ashley had run away from them to the other side of the playground. She sat alone and pulled her hood over her head. She'd only wanted to see what they were doing. But now she sat by herself until the bell rang. It seemed as if she always sat by herself, because there were no girls her age in her classroom.

Cindy's teacher took her to the principal, Mr. Aycox. Cindy had never been sent to his office before. He usually smiled when he saw her in the hall, but he did not smile today.

Soon another teacher came into the room. Mrs. Monaghan was the teacher for children with special needs, the class where Ashley was a student.

Cindy looked down while the grown-ups talked. She couldn't understand why they were making a big deal about that one little word, "retard." She heard other kids say it all the time—she just happened to get caught.

She began to pay attention again when she heard Mr. Aycox say, "Cindy, this kind of thing happens when people don't understand one another. We're going to arrange for you to spend some time in the class for children with special needs. How about a half hour a day for the next two weeks? Is that all right with you?"

"Yes," Cindy whispered, but she thought it sounded awful. How would she survive two whole weeks with those kids!

The next day Cindy came to the special-needs classroom. While Mrs. Monaghan introduced her, Ashley kept her head down. She felt angry. How could Mrs. Monaghan let that girl in their room—their safe, special room at Yates School? These were going to be two very long weeks!

Mrs. Monaghan sent the children to their desks. Then she took Cindy aside. "Let's talk for a minute," she said.

"What do you know about kids with special needs?"

Cindy shrugged and looked down.

"Not too much? Okay, I'll try to fill you in as we go along. How many adults are there in your fourth-grade room?"

"One," said Cindy in a very low voice.

"And how many kids?" asked Mrs. Monaghan. "Twenty-two," said Cindy.

"We have nine students and five adults. The other four adults are my helpers. Not at all like your class, is it?"

Cindy shook her head.

"We have so many adults in this room so that we can give the kids here the extra attention they need to learn," said Mrs. Monaghan. "These children learn best when they have lots of practice and time with their lessons.

"All of the children in this class have disabilities.

This means that they cannot do some important things that other kids their age can do, like read or spell or speak. You may know someone who cannot walk or hear. These are disabilities, too.

"Disabilities are caused by problems with the brain or body, called handicapping conditions. People either are born with conditions or get them through a bad accident or illness.

"So you see that it's not my students' fault that they have trouble learning. They want to do well, just like you do. And in this room, with all of these helpers, they can work as quickly or slowly as they need to. They are all working at different levels."

Mrs. Monaghan pointed to two boys in the class. "That's Frank with the light hair. He's eight. He needs tutoring in second-grade reading and math. That's Giresh with the black hair. He's also eight. We're helping him learn colors and counting."

Cindy wondered how the boys could be the same age and learning such different things, but she was too embarrassed to ask any questions.

After they had finished talking, it was free time for the class, and most of the kids played with toys. One boy ran and spun around the room. But Ashley sat alone at a window, wishing Cindy would leave.

A boy with red hair sat down next to Cindy with a box of blocks. "Hi, I'm Jesse," he said. "Want to play?"

"No," said Cindy. She wished she weren't there.

The next day Cindy saw a different teacher working with some of the class. The rest of the kids, including Ashley, were writing at their desks. Mrs. Monaghan introduced Cindy to Mrs. Fischer, the speech teacher. She told Cindy that the class might be doing something different each time she came.

Mrs. Fischer told the story of the Little Red Hen in words and sign language. Then she had the children make paper-bag puppets of the Little Red Hen. They cut out red beaks and glued them on the bags; then they made the sign for red.

The boy next to Cindy moved his hands as if he was trying to tell her something. Cindy didn't know what to do. She felt uncomfortable.

One of the helpers said, "Luis is asking you to help him glue the beak on his puppet."

Cindy did. *That was easy,* she thought.

At the end of the lesson, Mrs. Monaghan explained to Cindy that Mrs. Fischer came three times a week to help the children with talking.

"Why do they use sign language?" asked Cindy, "Are they deaf?"

"No, but for different reasons some of these kids can't speak very much, so they use a mix of words and signs. Not all the kids, though. Ashley, for instance, uses and *understands* words just as you do."

Cindy felt her face get red. She turned and hurried out the door.

Ashley and some other kids were leaving the classroom the next time Cindy came.

"Look, it's Cindy," said Frank.

Ashley looked away.

Cindy wondered where they were going. Mrs. Monaghan explained: "Many children in this class spend part of the day in regular-grade classrooms. There are some subjects they don't need extra help to learn. It's also important for them to work and play with children their own age. Jesse spends part of the day in the first-grade room, and Kyanna and Jeremy go to kindergarten. Ashley and Frank go to second grade for math, music, art, and gym.

"There are different ways children with special needs can be included in regular classes and activities. Getting them together with kids who do not have special needs is called mainstreaming. In fact," said Mrs. Monaghan, "many people think that the kids in my class should spend their whole day in a regular classroom. That's called inclusion, and it happens in some schools. But this is how it's done at our school—at least for now."

As Ashley's group walked out, six other kids came in and sat down on the rug with the rest of Mrs. Monaghan's class.

"These are first graders who come to this room for a half hour every day," said Mrs. Monaghan. "They're here, like you, to get to know the children in my room. We do lessons and games that will help all the kids listen and speak better. Would you like to join us?"

"No," said Cindy. "I'll watch."

Cindy wondered how Mrs. Monaghan could keep track of everyone coming and going. None of these kids had ever come to her classroom. And her class only left their room for lunch or special programs, and they all went together.

She watched the children practice sign language and play a listening game. Then they sang a song together. Cindy thought they looked happy.

Cindy had a question for Mrs. Monaghan. "Why is Ashley in this class instead of second grade if she can do second-grade work?"

"She can do some of it," said Mrs. Monaghan, "but not all. She has a handicapping condition called epilepsy. It got in the way of her learning when she was younger. She's in this room so she can catch up on the schoolwork she missed when her epilepsy was more of a problem. Eventually, she will be in a regular classroom full-time. Do you know what epilepsy is?"

"No."

"People with epilepsy have seizures sometimes. When Ashley has a seizure, her brain and nerves stop working the way they're supposed to. Her eyes stay open, but for about thirty seconds her body sort of shuts down, and she doesn't know what's happening around her.

"Her seizures don't hurt. In fact, she can't feel or think while they're happening. But she says that it's scary when a seizure is over. She feels as if she's just woken up and can't remember where she is or what she was just doing."

"That does sound scary. I didn't know that about her."

"Actually, her seizures are not as serious as they could be. There are different kinds of seizures. Some are very obvious because the person falls down and starts shaking. And they might last for minutes instead of seconds."

"But that doesn't happen to Ashley, does it?" asked Cindy.

"No," said Mrs. Monaghan. "It just seems as if she's staring into space. That's how her problems with school started. She wasn't born with epilepsy, as some children are. She started having seizures when she was about five or six. They may have been caused by an injury to her head, but no one is sure, and at first no one realized she was having them. They thought she was having problems paying attention. She was probably having seizures about ten times a day. That could really get in the way of your schoolwork, don't you think?"

"Yeah!" said Cindy.

"But now she takes medicine to prevent her from having as many seizures, though we must always keep an eye on her just in case she has one that makes her fall and hurt herself. And we help her work hard to make up the lessons she missed. But being in this class most of the day is not a perfect solution for Ashley. She misses chances to make good friends with girls her age."

"Oh," said Cindy, looking down at her hands. She remembered how Ashley had watched her and her friends on the playground.

shoelaces or a piece of yarn. Sometimes he held his fingers up and squinted at the light coming through them. He looked out the window a lot, too.

When Mrs. Monaghan noticed Cindy watching him, she said, "Would you like to ask me about Richard?"

Cindy's eyes followed him as he whirled and hummed around the room. "Yeah. Why does he do that?"

"It's one of his favorite things to do. He'd rather do that than play with a toy or be with other people. It's the way he was born. He has a handicapping condition called autism.

"Something about Richard's brain keeps him from understanding a lot of what's going on around him," Mrs. Monaghan continued. "Children with autism can see and hear as well as we do, but doctors think that the information they get from their eyes, ears, and other sensory organs is ignored or mixed up by their brains so they can't really understand it."

It was free time again when Cindy visited next. She watched Jeremy and Kyanna build with blocks. But then she couldn't help noticing Richard, a boy who was always running and spinning around the room.

Cindy hadn't ever heard him talk. He only made sounds and hummed songs—especially "Yankee Doodle." He didn't play with toys or with the other children at free time. Instead, he fiddled with his

"So that's why he doesn't pay attention?" asked Cindy.

"That's part of it. If your teacher stood on his head, would you notice?"

Cindy couldn't help giggling. "Yes!" she said.

"Well, Richard wouldn't. For some reason, what Richard feels inside as he spins around is much more interesting to him than anything I do. He rarely looks in people's eyes. Children with autism don't really seem to notice when other people are around them, perhaps because it is so difficult for them to understand what people say and do. But they seem to enjoy or even need to do things like spin, twist string, or hum. Doctors think they repeat these activities over and over again to give themselves the stimulation and comfort they can't get from listening to people or reacting to everything going on around them."

Mrs. Monaghan also explained that because

Richard doesn't notice what's happening outside of himself, he doesn't know about danger. He could touch a sharp object or run in the road without realizing he was doing something that could hurt him.

"That's why one adult in this room is always watching him. Many of the kids here need to be supervised all the time. That's part of the special attention they get. The other students try to protect Richard, too."

"Yes," said Cindy, "I saw that. It's funny, though, because he doesn't even seem to know they are there."

"Yes, that's true. But, you know, kids with autism can be very different from one another. Many don't understand what's going on around them, but some do. Some are very intelligent and can be in regular classrooms. But they still have to work very hard at paying attention to other people.

"There are also a few autistic children who, for reasons we don't understand, have incredible memories. They can play a song after hearing it just once or memorize a whole phone book. But with all this mental power, they could still have trouble talking with another person, because their brain might not process what that person was saying. Autism is extremely isolating—Richard is alone in his own world.

"But sometimes Richard seems to understand what we say. He may learn some words by the time he grows up, and he may not. He will never be like you and me."

"That's sad," said Cindy.

"Yes, it seems so," said Mrs. Monaghan. "But does he seem sad to you?"

"No, not at all," said Cindy.

"I don't think so, either."

On another day when Cindy came, she watched Jesse do math with Mrs. Monaghan. Jesse had a frown on his face as he gripped his pencil tightly. He sounded as if he was kicking his feet, too.

"I don't want to do any more!" he shouted.

"It's okay, Jesse," said Mrs. Monaghan as she put her hand over his. "We're almost finished."

"But I don't want to finish!"

"I think you can do it after a short rest. While you're resting, can I tell Cindy how hard you work?"

"Yes!" said Jesse.

"Cindy, Jesse has trouble sitting still at a desk and settling down to work. His emotions are very strong, and he gets upset easily, as he did just now. Right, Jesse?"

"Yeah," said Jesse, sitting with his arms folded and a frown on his face.

"I know not to be angry with him when he is like this. There are big long words for Jesse's condition. It's called Attention Deficit Hyperactivity Disorder. Isn't that a mouthful? Most people call it ADHD for short. It means Jesse has a lot of energy and problems paying attention. He's also impulsive—he has trouble stopping himself from doing things he knows he's not supposed to. Of course, he has to take the consequences when he does, but it's my job to stay calm and remind him to try to think ahead. I also help him learn to pay attention to his schoolwork."

"But Mrs. Monaghan," said Cindy, "I have trouble paying attention, too."

"Everybody does, sometimes. But for Jesse, it's harder. Can you imagine—every single minute his brain is telling him things like 'Oh, what's that noise? Hey, I can make a sound with my feet— *clomp, clomp, clomp!* Is it time for gym yet? And what's my teacher, the one who never stops talking, saying now?' How would you ever get your work done if your mind was distracting you like that?"

Cindy and Jesse laughed. He unfolded his arms and gave Mrs. Monaghan a hug.

"Well, it's tough. Your brain, Cindy, blocks out distractions so you can concentrate. It doesn't pay attention to the top of your desk or the color of your pencil as you write. It shuts out the noise of other kids whispering or scraping their chairs while your teacher is talking. But Jesse's brain gives equal attention to everything. Doctors don't really understand why this happens to some kids. It has nothing to do with how smart they may be. In fact, some kids with ADHD have grown up to be very accomplished people. They have so much energy that, once they learn how to use it, they can be great at whatever job they want to do.

"For now, Jesse goes to a doctor, and he takes medicine to help him focus on one thing at a time and to settle down. He and his parents and I are working on ways he can learn to calm himself. Right, buddy? Now, are you ready to try again?"

"Okay. And Mrs. Monaghan, it's free time next, right?" asked Jesse.

"Right," she answered.

During the break, Cindy played with the puppets. She sang softly as her puppets danced.

Ashley watched from the other side of the room. *She likes puppets,* she thought. *Just like I do.*

When Cindy arrived the next day, the kids were having a morning meeting. She sat at a desk and watched. They began by singing a "hello song" and shaking hands.

Cindy saw how everyone, even the kids who did not use many spoken words, helped with the meeting. Jesse took attendance. Marcos held up the weather pictures. Giresh did the calendar. And Luis showed the letters for the alphabet song.

Mrs. Monaghan helped each child in a different way. She helped some children read words. She helped others say sounds.

Cindy noticed that Jeremy was having a problem today. He didn't want to shake hands during the hello song. Then he talked loudly when he wasn't supposed to. He jabbed Marcos and Jesse with his elbow, then started kicking everyone around him. Mrs. Monaghan asked all the children to move away. She held Jeremy on the floor while he kicked and screamed so that he wouldn't hurt himself or anyone else.

Mrs. Monaghan talked to him in a calm voice, saying things like "I know you're angry, Jeremy. When you've settled down, you can tell me what the problem is. You don't have to kick and hit. I know you're upset. I will start letting you go, Jeremy, as soon as you stop kicking and hitting."

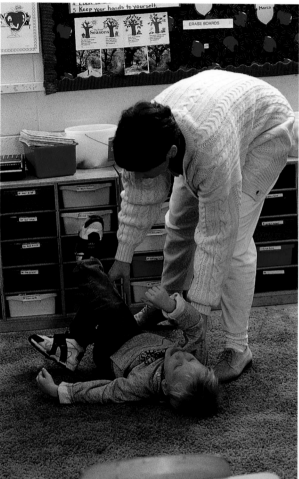

The other children waited. A few watched or talked quietly. Giresh looked at a book. Suddenly, Jesse ran up to comfort his teacher. He put his arms around her and said, "I love you, Mrs. Monaghan." Then he ran back to his seat.

Finally, Jeremy started to settle down. His teacher let go of him one arm and leg at a time.

Two of the adult helpers led him to his desk. Mrs. Monaghan was still calm. She went on with the meeting.

Later, Mrs. Monaghan said to Cindy, "Learning self-control is what some kids in here really need help with. You have a two-year-old brother, don't you?"

"Yes."

"Does he ever act the way Jeremy just did?"

Cindy laughed. "He sure does. He's crazy."

"No, he's not," said Mrs. Monaghan with a smile. "It's normal for a two-year-old to have tantrums. As kids get older, they learn to control their feelings and use words to get what they want. Jeremy's taking longer to do that. His mother and I are working together to get him to talk about what he wants instead of having temper tantrums. We try to do the same thing every time he has a problem. This helps calm him down more quickly. Still, I realize it might have been scary for you to watch."

"I was a little worried," said Cindy, "but you seemed to know exactly what to do."

"Yes, I learned when I trained to be a teacher. But Jeremy has to figure out how to calm himself down. If he doesn't, he could have big trouble as an adult. Can you imagine someone my size kicking and screaming around this room? It wouldn't be very pretty, would it?"

"Not at all!" said Cindy.

"Actually, Jeremy has other things to work on besides self-control. He also has trouble speaking and moving around. He is new to our class, so I'm still figuring out what problems he has, but I believe he has more than one condition. There is a name for that: 'multiply-handicapped.'"

"Oh," said Cindy. "But I thought 'handicapped' meant someone in a wheelchair."

"That's true. But 'handicapped' is another word for 'disabled.' You remember that a disability prevents kids from doing something that other kids their age can do. Not just walking or running, but also reading, writing, thinking, speaking, or learning self-control.

"But the words 'handicapped' and 'disabled,' and all the names of conditions that I've taught you—autism, epilepsy, ADHD—are labels. Labels belong in stores on boxes of raisin bran. Sticking labels on real people with real feelings is a silly thing to do. I mean, would you like to be known as 'Cindy, the multiply-handicapped kid,' if you had the same problems as Jeremy?"

"No, I would *not* like it," said Cindy.

"There is a lot more to Jeremy than his problems, but we do have to use labels sometimes to give information. For example, I needed to tell you about autism so you wouldn't feel uncomfortable about Richard's spinning around the room. Labels can also help teachers know how to help a child. But, in general, they are sort of silly and sometimes just plain rude."

Ashley didn't like it—she didn't like it at all. Cindy was in the room again. And she was hanging around Mrs. Monaghan, as usual. Ashley snuggled closer to her helper, Mrs. Rosenbaum.

Today Cindy was watching Mrs. Monaghan do a lesson with Frank.

"So," said Mrs. Monaghan, "let's finish correcting that math page. We're on the last row. Should I cover up the rest of the page again so you don't get distracted? Or should we leave the paper off now?"

"Leave it off. Mrs. Monaghan, are we going outside today?"

"Focus, Frank, we're doing math now. What row are we on?"

"Uh, I don't know. Oh yeah, the last row."

"Go for it, sport," said Mrs. Monaghan.

"Sixteen plus twenty-one is…"

"Look again," said Mrs. Monaghan. "What are the numbers you're adding?"

"Oh! Sixteen plus *twelve* is…twenty-eight!"

"Right!"

knows how to add and subtract, but he often gets the wrong answers for other reasons. Usually, he mixes up the order of the numbers he's adding, so he sees 12 as 21 and 34 as 43. When this happens, even if he adds correctly, he'll get the wrong answer."

"Mmm," said Cindy. "I do that sometimes, but..."

"But probably not as often. Frank has a learning disability. Kids with learning disabilities have trouble with the way their brain handles some of the information it gets. Things like the shape and order of numbers, letters, or words get scrambled up for them. And for some of these kids it is hard to remember directions in the right order. This makes schoolwork difficult, even though they are just as smart as other kids their age."

Cindy watched as Frank finished the page. Then Mrs. Monaghan worked with him at the chalkboard. He wrote a row of numbers from one to ten. Some were missing; others were backward. Mrs. Monaghan wrote the row the correct way. Frank wrote more rows and tried to concentrate on making all the numbers face the right direction.

"Great job, kid!" said Mrs. Monaghan. "You're done for now."

"I guess math is kind of hard for Frank," said Cindy as she watched him go to the art area.

"Actually, it's not," said Mrs. Monaghan. "He

"How do you get a learning disability?" Cindy wanted to know.

"It's really hard to say," said Mrs. Monaghan. "A child could have an injury or illness that hurts the brain, or he could just be born this way."

Cindy asked, "Does having a learning disability bother Frank?"

"It can, when people make him feel bad about not getting the right answer. But with special help and a lot of attention, kids with learning disabilities are able to do the same work as kids in regular classrooms."

"Can his problem get fixed?"

"No, but I can figure out ways he can learn the same things you do. That's why Frank is here, so I can remind him to concentrate and give him small amounts of work to do at a time. And I can teach him to check words and numbers twice, and to make lists when he needs to remember to do things in a certain order. Tricks like these will help him to manage his problem himself when he grows up."

When Cindy came,
she often watched
Luis. He was the boy
she had helped with
gluing on her second
day in the classroom.

Cindy noticed that Luis did not speak except to
say, "Pa." Yet he seemed to understand many
words in both English and Spanish. He had beauti-
ful eyes and a face that seemed to tell so many
words and feelings.

"Did you know, Cindy," said Mrs. Monaghan,
"that Luis is nine, the same age you are? He is
learning to name colors, count from one to five,
and trace his name."

"What handicapping condition does he have?"
asked Cindy.

"He has Down syndrome.

never speak well is because his brain did not grow the way it should. Like all children with Down syndrome, he cannot learn and understand information like other kids his age, and he will never catch up. Still, he works very hard, and eventually he may learn some words. Each child with Down syndrome is affected differently. Some are able to speak well, but others cannot do the things Luis can do—like walk and feed himself. So they might have to live in a hospital where they can be cared for all the time.

"Did you know that the word 'retarded' means 'slowed down'? Some people use it to be hurtful. But what 'retarded' really means is that a person has been held back from a regular life by a body and brain with serious problems."

Cindy muttered something.

"What?" asked Mrs. Monaghan.

"I didn't know what that word meant," said Cindy.

"I figured you didn't. Anyone who knows or loves a person who is retarded doesn't use that word carelessly. It's too sad when you know what it really means."

"Down syndrome is a condition that some babies are born with that keeps them from developing as they should. You know a baby has Down syndrome right after birth because his eyes, nose, and ears have a slightly different shape. But also parts of his body—like his lungs, heart, and ears—are not fully formed, so he'll tend to have a lot of medical problems. Luis has tubes in his ears to help him hear."

"Oh, is that why he can't talk?" asked Cindy.

"Well, it doesn't help. But the real reason he will

Cindy looked down. "It is sad, because there's something really nice about Luis...."

"I know what you mean," said Mrs. Monaghan. "The kids I know with Down syndrome are usually very loving and special people. But I don't think you need to feel sorry for Luis. He doesn't seem to get easily frustrated, even though the simplest activities can be hard for him. I think he's happy. And he likes to make other people happy, too."

Luis was busy with the puppets now. Cindy went to sit with him. Ashley was also playing with the puppets. She was having so much fun with them that she didn't notice that it was Cindy who was sitting next to her. When

Ashley looked over, Cindy smiled at her. Ashley got up and quickly walked away.

On the playground the next day, Cindy saw Ashley sitting alone, watching other kids climb on the bars. She noticed Ashley every day now.

When Cindy went into the classroom later, Mrs. Monaghan said, "I think this is a good day to send you out of the room with a group. Marcos, Giresh, and Jeremy are on their way to PT, which is short for *physical therapy*. It's a special exercise class they go to twice a week."

Cindy went with the boys and the two physical therapists, Jeff and Peggy, to a room in the basement. First, the students did sit-ups. Cindy held Jeremy's feet.

"Good job!" said Cindy when it was time to stop.

"Too hard!" said Jeremy.

Next, Jeff and Peggy made an obstacle course. The boys had to jump over a rope, walk a short balance beam, and match large plastic shapes.

Then they stood on pieces of carpet and slid around the room or sat on a little seat with wheels and rolled along. Cindy watched and sometimes helped.

Later, back in the classroom, Mrs. Monaghan asked, "How was PT?"

"Pretty interesting," said Cindy. "It's like gym class."

"Yes, in a way it is. You see, a lot of these kids need extra help with moving and coordinating their bodies. They need more help than they could get in a regular gym class. Jeff and Peggy choose special exercises for each child. Marcos, who has Down syndrome—like Luis—has problems walking because of his weak muscles and sense of balance. Those stairs you run up and down every day are difficult for him to climb. The physical therapists give him exercises that strengthen his muscles and make him practice moving steadily and smoothly. That helps him feel more comfortable on the stairs, the playground, and everywhere else."

30

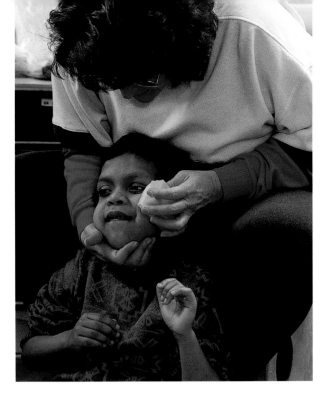

work. It is hard to do an assignment if you have trouble holding a pencil or scissors, or following the teacher's instructions.

"Remember what I said the other day about Marcos and Down syndrome? Some conditions like that cause children to have weak muscles. The activities in OT and PT get them to use the muscles in their bodies and hands so they grow stronger."

Mrs. Monaghan explained that Miss Bonnie, the occupational therapist, often started the lesson by pressing or brushing muscles in the kids' arms, faces, or shoulders. This loosened their muscles so they would work better during the activity.

"Hi, Mrs. Monaghan, how are you?"

"Hello, Cindy. I guess you're getting used to us. Just in time for your last day. We'll have you say good-bye to the class before you leave. Right now, you might want to watch the kids having occupational therapy, otherwise known as OT."

"What's OT?" asked Cindy.

"Well, it's a little like physical therapy. In PT, kids practice moving their bodies so they can get around the school more easily. Occupational therapy gives them practice using their hands and following directions so they can do their school-

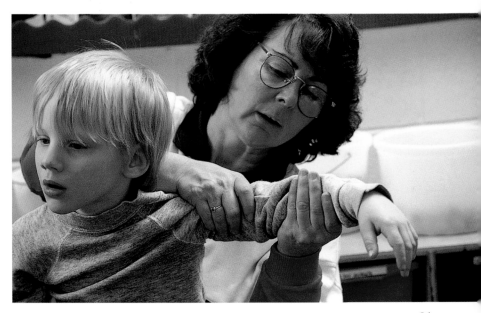

"What kind of things do they do?" asked Cindy.

"They might cook from a recipe, string beads in patterns, or play with a parachute—all activities that use their hands! Today they are tracing one another's bodies on big sheets of paper."

Cindy watched. Marcos was tracing Kyanna.

"That's me!" said Kyanna when Marcos was done. "I guess I'm really big!"

Miss Bonnie collected all the tracings. She told the kids they could cut them out and color them tomorrow. While she talked, Ms. Scott, the art teacher, was setting up a clay project.

Mrs. Monaghan told Cindy, "Art is really important for these kids. Just like OT, it gives them good practice using their hands and following directions. And they love art. Just watch their faces as they do this project."

Cindy did watch.

She felt sad that some of the kids couldn't do everything she could do, but it made her smile to see how happy they were now, making things from clay.

Cindy whispered in Mrs. Monaghan's ear. Then she left without saying good-bye.

Ashley watched her walk out the door and smiled.

When Cindy walked into the classroom the next day, Ashley looked up in surprise. *What is she doing here?* Ashley wondered.

Mrs. Monaghan called the kids and had them sit on the rug in front of her. "Cindy has decided that she likes this class and all of you. She wants to keep coming to visit us."

What! Ashley couldn't believe it! How could Cindy like them after she had been so mean?

"She's been a really good friend," said Mrs. Monaghan. "Let's give her a clap for doing such a great job here."

Everyone clapped except Ashley.

"And give yourselves a clap for welcoming her into our classroom. Sometimes it's hard to give new people a chance."

They all clapped again. Ashley tried hard not to cry.

When the kids were back in their seats, Ashley felt someone touch her. It was her teacher. "I think you need to give her another chance," said Mrs. Monaghan.

Ashley kept her head down on her desk. "But she's one of the other kids. Why does she have to come here?"

"Ashley, there are no other kids. Just kids."

Ashley didn't lift her head. "I want to like her, but what if she doesn't like me back?"

"Give it a try when you're ready. You'll see, it's going to be okay."

Ashley didn't know what to do. She would be sad in her class every day now, not just for two weeks.

Soon it was time to go out to the playground. Ashley pulled on her hood and zipped up her jacket. She raced as fast as she could to her usual spot. There were tears in her eyes, and she wasn't paying attention, so she ran right into a group of kids.

"Hey, watch it!" said one girl. All four kids looked hard at Ashley. One of the boys said, "What class are *you* in?"

"Hey, *what?*" said another voice. It was Cindy. "Ashley's in the class for children with special needs, where I go sometimes. And she's my friend. You got a problem with that?"

The kids looked at one another and shrugged. They walked away.

Cindy sat down with Ashley. "They just don't know about your class, like I didn't before."

"I know," said Ashley. And she smiled at Cindy. "Thanks."

Ashley didn't sit with her hood over her face now. She watched some of the second-grade girls playing. She didn't get too close—yet. But one of these days she might join them.

AFTERWORD

As the author and photographer of this book, I was honored to look into the lives of the children at Yates School. This story is based on a true incident that happened there. Cindy and Ashley were not the two kids involved, but they agreed to act it out for me. All the others in the book acted as themselves.

There are many conditions I did not talk about in this book. (On page 40, I have listed some additional sources of information.) I wrote about those I found in this particular special-needs class. Often when the words "disabilities," "handicaps," or "special needs" are used, kids might picture someone in a wheelchair. That is a physical handicap. You might know about others, such as blindness or deafness.

The children in this class, though, have disabilities that you cannot see easily because they are hidden in their bodies within the brain and nervous system. A little background on how the brain and nervous system handle information can help you begin to understand these children's conditions.

The nervous system is a sort of communication network made up of thin fibers that are everywhere in your body. The fibers are made of nerve cells, or neurons. These neurons send information to your brain from every part of your body. They connect your perceptions—everything you see, touch, taste, smell, and hear—with the nervous-system command center in your brain. Neurons in the brain process the information they receive and then send signals back along the nerve fibers to tell parts of your body how to react.

Neurons in the brain and body pass along information through an electrochemical reaction. When your eyes, ears, or other sensory organs perceive something, a chain reaction starts. A chemical is released at one end of a neuron, which begins a mini-electrical reaction within the cell. This causes another chemical to be released at the other end of the neuron. The chemical jumps across a small space to the next neuron, which then repeats the process. And so the chemical reaction travels along a pathway all the way to your brain, carrying information about something you saw, heard, felt, tasted, or smelled. The chemicals that help carry this information are called neurotransmitters; they are very important in helping the nervous system function correctly.

Here is a simplified example of how this process works. Imagine you are taking a spelling test and your teacher says the word "incredible." Your ears hear the sound, and the neurons there flash tiny electrical signals along a pathway to your brain. *Incredible*, you think, as you try to remember what the word looked like on that crumpled spelling list. Your brain is translating these signals into a word. It is comparing the word "incredible" to other words you have stored in your memory, searching for the right match. *Okay, I think I've got it*, you say to yourself. Now neurons flash electrical signals back from your brain, through your body, to your fingers so you can pick up your pencil and start writing the word. Information is also traveling in neurons back and forth from your eyes and brain as you look at what you write and try to decide whether or not the word seems correct. It does. *Whew, that's right*, you think. Neurons send signals from your brain to your mouth, and you smile. And all of this happens in seconds!

As you can see, this is a very quick and complicated process, involving billions of neurons working together. And if some of these neurons are not working correctly, then the information is lost or garbled and you cannot spell "incredible."

This is what happens for many children with special needs. Information from different parts of their bodies may not travel correctly along the neuron pathways. Therefore, it doesn't get to the brain. Or it might make it there, but for some reason the brain cannot translate the signals. Or maybe it does translate, but the nervous system doesn't send the information back to the parts of the body so they can react.

What conditions like autism, ADHD (Attention Deficit Hyperactivity Disorder), epilepsy, and learning disabilities have in common is that they are caused by problems with the brain and nervous system. What is different about each condition is exactly how the brain and nervous system are affected.

For example, Ashley has an epileptic seizure when a group of neurons in her brain start sending their signals, or firing, wildly all at once. This is not normal, because they are supposed to send signals in a very organized way, and only with a purpose, such as giving information to your hands, eyes, or ears. This wild and repeated firing overloads Ashley's system so that for a short period of time her body and brain can't communicate with each other and she may lose consciousness.

Jesse's condition, ADHD, is caused by a different nervous-system problem. Although it has not been proved, many doctors believe that ADHD is caused by slight imbalances in the chemicals, or neurotransmitters, produced in the front of the brain. The neurons in these frontal lobes control your emotions, your ability to pay attention, and how active you are, so any disturbances there would greatly affect your behavior.

Frank's learning disability is, in some ways, similar to Jesse's ADHD. Doctors think that learning disabilities are also caused by slight imbalances in neurotransmitter chemicals. However, different chemicals and different sets of neurons are involved.

A child with a learning disability is most likely to have trouble with the neurons in the parts of the brain that control higher learning.

Although their conditions are different, a child with ADHD and one with learning disabilities might behave similarly in school. A child with a learning disability might become frustrated with his lessons and stop paying attention. And if people were annoyed with him because he wasn't learning quickly, he might become angry and seem as if he couldn't control his emotions, just like a child with ADHD.

Likewise, a child with ADHD, even though the higher-learning parts of his brain worked well, could have so much trouble focusing and sitting still that he would not be able to finish his lessons and so appear to have a learning disability.

You can see from this example that different conditions can cause children to have similar problems in school. In fact, all of the ones mentioned in this book, no matter how different, prevent children from learning as well as they should, which is why these kids are in a class for children with special needs.

It is important to note that not all children with handicapping conditions have to be in a special-needs class. Also, some schools do not have separate classrooms for children who do have special needs. Instead, the regular classroom teacher and extra helpers work with them. Including these children in a regular classroom is called "inclusion," and some people believe this is how all special education will soon be handled in this country. Finding opportunities to mix students with special needs and those in regular classes—as shown here at Yates School—is a step in that direction.

Most people do not object to inclusion, but some worry about whether or not children with disabilities can get the attention they need in a regular classroom. This is especially true for conditions such as Down syndrome and autism. They are usually more serious than learning disabilities and ADHD. The children who have them—like Luis, Marcos, and Richard —need a lot of special help.

Doctors believe that autism affects neurons throughout the brain. Richard has so much trouble learning because so many of his information-handling neurons are not able to work correctly.

Down syndrome is different from these other conditions because it affects many parts of the child's brain *and* body. From the moment a Down-syndrome child like Luis comes into being inside his mother, there is a problem with the special cells, or genes, that tell his body how to develop. Because of this, many parts—including his brain—simply do not get the orders to grow as they should. A child with Down syndrome will never be able to learn all of the things that other children his age can, plus he may have trouble with physical activities.

Doing this book gave me great respect for what many of us take for granted: a "normally" functioning brain, nervous system, and body. Many of us work hard at something special— sports, music, schoolwork, or art—and we do well not only because we try hard, but also because we are healthy. The children I photographed and wrote about here work just as hard as you do, but sometimes their bodies and brains just won't cooperate. They deserve respect, friendliness, and extra support so that they, too, can achieve.

—**ELLEN B. SENISI**

BIBLIOGRAPHY and SOURCES

Batshaw, Mark L., M.D., and Yvonne M. Perret, M.A., M.S.W., L.C.S.W. *Children with Disabilities: A Medical Primer.* Baltimore: Paul H. Brookes Publishing Company, 1992.

Greenfeld, Josh. *A Place for Noah.* New York: Holt, Rinehart and Winston, 1978.

Hall, David E., M.D. *Living with Learning Disabilities: A Guide for Students.* Minneapolis: Lerner Publications Company, 1993.

Hart, Charles A. *A Parent's Guide to Autism: Answers to the Most Common Questions.* New York: Pocket Books, 1993.

Ingersoll, Barbara, Ph.D. *Your Hyperactive Child: A Parent's Guide to Coping with Attention Deficit Disorder.* New York: Doubleday, 1988.

Naparstek, Nathan, Ph.D. *The Learning Solution: What to Do If Your Child Has Trouble with Schoolwork.* New York: Avon Books, 1993.

Silver, Larry B., M.D. *The Misunderstood Child: A Guide for Parents of Learning Disabled Children.* New York: McGraw-Hill, 1984.

The Down Syndrome World Wide Web Page: http://www.nas.com/downsyn/